BIG RED BATH

To Theo William and Maya Josephine — J.J.

For Rebecca Anne — A.R.

ORCHARD BOOKS
338 Euston Road, London NW1 3BH
Orchard Books Australia
Level 17/207 Kent Street, Sydney, NSW 2000
First published in 2004 by Orchard Books
First published in paperback in 2005
ISBN 978 1 84362 605 3
Text © Julia Jarman 2004
Illustrations © Adrian Reynolds 2004
The rights of Julia Jarman to be identified as the author
and Adrian Reynolds to be identified as the illustrator
of this work have been asserted by them in accordance
with the Copyright, Designs and Patents Act, 1988.
A CIP catalogue record for this book is available from the British Library.
10
Printed in China
Orchard Books is a division of Hachette Children's Books,
an Hachette UK company.
www.hachette.co.uk

JULIA JARMAN & ADRIAN REYNOLDS
BIG RED BATH

ORCHARD BOOKS

Ben and Bella in the big red bath —
"Splash you!"
"Splash you!"

Splish! Splosh! Splash!
Bubbles in the bath.
Water on the floor.

But who's this
scratching at the door?

"Hi there, kids! Can I come for a swim?"
"Course you can, Dog. Just dive in!"

Dog dives in, front feet first.

Bubbles rise, bubbles burst!

Dog, Ben and Bella in the big red bath –
"Splash you!"
"Splash you!"

Splish!

Splosh!

Splash!

Bubbles in the bath.
Water on the floor.

But who's this roaring
at the door?

"Hi there, kids! Can I have a wash?"
"Leap in, Lion. Splish and splosh!"

Lion leaps in and starts to scrub.

Bubbles rise — rub-a-dub-dub!

Lion and Dog, Ben and Bella in the bath —
"Splash you!"
"Splash you!"

"Hello, kids! Can I come for a paddle?"
"Course you can, Duck! Dibble and dabble!"

Duck dibble-dabbles at a quacking pace.

Bubbles fly all over the place!

Duck, Lion and Dog, Ben and Bella in the bath —
"Splash you!"
"Splash you!"

Turtle hurtles in,
"Can I have a dip?"

Pursued by Penguin,
"I want to flip!"

Giraffe races in,
"Make room for me.
I'm being followed!"

Who can it be?

It's Hippopotamus!

He slips on the floor!

He slides under the bath —

which goes

sloosh

through the door and . . .

...down the stairs — so very fast!
Kangaroo wants a ride
but the bath shoots past!

But Kanga's determined!
She takes a bound —
so the big red bath suddenly . . .

...leaves the **ground!**

It flies twice round the world,
over mountain and plain —

till a flock of flamingos . . .

. . . tows it home again!

Bubbles in the bath.
Water on the floor.
Who is **this** coming in the door?

"It's Mum!"
Rubba-dubba-giggle,
rubba-dubba-laugh.

"Let's tell Mum about
our big red bath!"